Little Red Robin

D0317094

Do you have all the Little Red Robin books?

- ☐ Buster's Big Surprise
- ☐ The Purple Butterfly
- ☐ How Bobby Got His Pet
- ☐ We are Super!
- ☐ New Friends
- ☐ Robo-Robbie

Also available as ebooks

Little Red
Robin

Robo-Robbie

Chae Strathie
Illustrated by Mark Marshall
SCHOLASTIC

For Joseph and Mairead

Scholastic Children's Books
An imprint of Scholastic Ltd
Euston House, 24 Eversholt Street
London, NW1 1DB, UK
Registered office: Westfield Road, Southam, Warwickshire, CV47 0RA
SCHOLASTIC and associated logos are trademarks and/or registered
trademarks of Scholastic Inc.

First published in 2014 by Scholastic Ltd

Text copyright © Chae Strathie, 2014
Illustrations © Mark Marshall, 2014

The rights of Chae Strathie and Mark Marshall
to be identified as the author and illustrator of
this work have been asserted by them.

ISBN 978 1407 13886 2

A CIP catalogue record for this book is available from the British Library

Printed in China.

1 3 5 7 9 10 8 6 4 2

www.scholastic.co.uk/zone

Chapter One

Robbie's dad was an inventor.

He invented fantastic things like the Clockwork
Candy-Floss Machine – which turned fresh air
into delicious clouds of scrumptiousness.

But Dad's inventions often ended up with loud
explosions and angry neighbours.

The worst time was when the HoverHoovie floating vacuum cleaner went crazy.

It sucked up hundreds of hats,

a small dog . . .

and Mayor Bumbleweed's bushy moustache.

So, when Dad called Robbie into his workshop one Saturday afternoon, Robbie knew he had to be ready for anything.

He put on his swimming goggles,

his BMX helmet . . .

and his raincoat.

Then he cautiously opened the door. . .

Chapter Two

"Robbie," said Dad excitedly, "meet Robbie."

Robbie couldn't believe his eyes.

There, looking back at him, was . . . himself.

"This," said Dad proudly, "is the Robo-Robbie ZX1."

"Hello, Robbie," said the robot in an identical voice to his. "How are you today?"

"Err, fine . . . thanks," replied Robbie. "Dad, why have you made a robot that looks like me?"

"I'm entering the World Robot Championships," said Dad. "He's the bee's knees, isn't he?"

Dad always said things like that. If he thought something was brilliant, he said it was the bee's knees or the cat's pyjamas or even the sardine's whiskers.

"He's amazing," said Robbie. "What can he do?"

"Let me show you," replied Dad, smiling.

Chapter Three

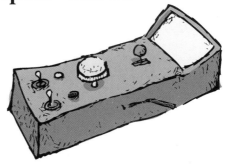

Dad picked up a black box from the table. It had several buttons on it, and a small screen.

Dad pressed a large silver button in the middle and Robo-Robbie marched out of the workshop into the back garden.

Robbie and Dad followed him.

When Robo-Robbie reached the shed, he didn't stop – he walked right up one side of it, over the roof and down the other side.

"Not bad," said Robbie.

Next Dad flicked a switch.

With a puff of smoke, Robo-Robbie shot into the air and flew a loop-the-loop over their heads.

"If you look at the screen you'll see what he sees," said Dad.

Robbie peered at the small screen. Sure enough, through Robo-Robbie's eyes, he could see himself and Dad standing below. He could also see a big apple tree straight ahead.

"Don't worry," said Dad. "I programmed Robo-Robbie not to crash into things."

CRASH!

Robo-Robbie flew right into the tree.

"He may need a bit more work," Dad added.

Robbie and Dad untangled Robo-Robbie from the branches and took him back to the workshop.

"Now, you're absolutely not allowed to play with the robot," said Dad firmly as he pressed Robo-Robbie's nose to turn him off.

Robo-Robbie giggled, said "Bananatrumpet!" and switched off with a whirr.

"Bananatrumpet?" said Robbie.

"Ah, yes," said Dad. "He usually makes sense, but sometimes he comes out with complete gibberish. I'll fix that tomorrow."

Chapter Four

The next morning Robbie awoke early. He had hardly slept for thinking about all the fun he could have with his robot lookalike.

Everyone else in the house was still fast asleep, so Robbie crept downstairs, through the kitchen and into the workshop. . .

When Mum and Dad got up and came downstairs, Robbie was already sitting at the kitchen table.

"You're up early," said Mum, yawning. "What would you like for breakfast?"

"Cornbubbles," said Robbie.

"Cornbubbles? Is that a new cereal?" said Mum. "Never heard of them. You'll just have to have cornflakes."

Luckily Dad didn't seem to notice.

Because, of course, it wasn't the real Robbie sitting at the table – it was Robo-Robbie!

In the workshop, Robbie watched what was happening on the screen.

"Silly robot," he said. "What on earth are cornbubbles?"

After breakfast, Robbie pressed a button and Robo-Robbie asked, "Can I go out to play in the park?"

"OK, dear," said Mum. "Dad and I are going shopping in a while, but we won't be long."

Robo-Robbie waved and trotted out of the house.

"Now for some fun," chuckled Robbie.

Chapter Five

Robbie flicked a switch and Robo-Robbie blasted off into the sky.

Robbie could see everything that Robo-Robbie saw on the screen. He had a bird's eye view of the town below.

He spotted a football game in the park. Some small boys were trying to play, but a gang of older boys were stopping them.

"We'll see about that," muttered Robbie, steering Robo-Robbie down to the ground.

"Hey! Give me a go," said Robo-Robbie, running over.

"No way, pipsqueak," said the biggest boy, a bully called Bogie Boggart.

Back in the workshop, Robbie twisted a silver knob.

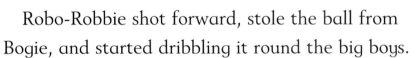

Robo-Robbie shot forward, stole the ball from Bogie, and started dribbling it round the big boys.

Faster and faster he went, until he was just a blur. Bogie and his gang tried to tackle Robo-Robbie, but they were way too slow.

Finally Robbie flicked a switch and Robo-Robbie's foot shot forward.

He blasted the ball so hard it rocketed from one end of the field to the other. It ripped a hole in the goals, knocked down several trees like dominoes and bounced down the hill out of sight.

"Oops," Robo-Robbie said.

"Hey!" cried one of the small boys. "That was my new ball!"

"Sorry," said Robo-Robbie. "I was just trying to help."

"Time to go," said Robbie as the big boys ran at Robo-Robbie. He turned a green knob and Robo-Robbie ran out of the park and towards the high street with the bullies chasing after him.

Chapter Six

Robo-Robbie sprinted round the corner into the high street. He needed to get out of sight of the bullies, before Robbie could make him fly home.

But there were too many people in the high street – they would notice if Robo-Robbie suddenly started flying! And the bullies were following right behind him.

Quick! Robo-Robbie needed to hide somewhere.

The first shop in the street was Madame Fifi's Fabulous Cake Emporium.

Robbie steered Robo-Robbie in through the door and hid him behind a huge display of chocolate eclairs.

Bogie was first to reach the shop. He started whistling, acting like he was just looking at the cakes.

But Robbie knew he was really looking for Robo-Robbie!

He had to do something. Fast.

"I wonder what this purple lever does?" Robbie said.

He pulled it . . . and Robo-Robbie began spinning round at high speed.

"Oh, no! How do I stop him?" Robbie said. He pressed a yellow button . . .

and Robo-Robbie's arms shot out like extra-long telescopes.

"That's not good," said Robbie.

Whirling round the shop like a rocket-powered windmill, Robo-Robbie sent cakes, cream, chocolate and jam flying everywhere.

A shower of sticky,
cakey mess splattered
out of the shop door.

Bogie and the other
bullies were covered
in gloop.

But rather than
getting even angrier,
their eyes lit up.

Being covered in cake
was much more fun than
fighting. Soon they were
all cheering and slurping
away happily.

The grown-ups on the high street looked much less happy.

Panicking, Robbie hit several buttons at once.

"Hootenanny!" Robo-Robbie shouted, he did a jig and super-kicked an enormous jam doughnut out of the door.

It soared past Robbie's mum and dad, who were doing the shopping, and – SPLAT! – hit Mayor Bumbleweed right in the face.

"Pants," said Robbie.

Chapter Seven

The mayor did not look happy at all.

"I hope you're going to give this young scallywag a good telling off," he harrumphed. "My lovely new moustache is covered in jam."

"Of course," said Mum sternly. "He's been very naughty."

"I think it's time we went home," said Dad. Then he added quietly, "Don't you, Robo-Robbie?"

"Robbie," said Dad, leading him to the naughty step, "didn't I tell you NOT to touch the robot?"

"Yes," said Robbie, looking at his feet.

They were back at the house.

"You," said Dad, wagging his finger, "have been a very, VERY naughty cheesepuff."

"A naughty what?" said Robbie.

"I – I mean, you've been a very twinkly shampoodle!"

"I hardly think this is the time for nonsense," said Mum.

"Banjopants!" yelped Dad as he tried to push a banana into his ear.

"Dad," said Robbie. "Why do you have steam coming out of your ears?"

"And sparks shooting out of your head?" asked Mum.

"Wait a minute," said Robbie suspiciously.
"You're not Dad . . . you're ROBO-DAD!"

The kitchen door slowly opened.

Dad had his dressing gown on and was holding a black controller, just like the one Robbie had been using for Robo-Robbie.

"I knew it!" said Robbie.

"Well?" said Mum sternly. "This had better
be good."

"I just wanted a lie-in," mumbled Dad sheepishly.
"And to get out of going shopping."

"Right," said Mum. "In that case, for setting
such a bad example, YOU can go on the naughty
step instead of Robbie."

"Now that," said Robbie, "is the bee's knees!"

"I think I'll invent something else next time," said Dad as he sulked on the naughty step. "Robots are far too much bother."